TOM'S PIRATE SHIP

A Spot-the-Difference Book

TOM'S PIRATE SHIP

BY
PHILIPPE DUPASQUIER

Ⓐ

Andersen Press · London

TOM'S PIRATE SHIP

A Spot-the-Difference Book

For the children of Dallington School

Copyright © 1993 by Philippe Dupasquier.
This paperback edition first published in 2003 by Andersen Press Ltd.
The rights of Philippe Dupasquier to be identified as the author and illustrator of this work
have been asserted by him in accordance with the Copyright, Designs and Patents Act, 1988. First
published in Great Britain in 1993 by Andersen Press Ltd. 20 Vauxhall Bridge Road, London SW1V 2SA.
Published in Australia by Random House Australia Pty., 20 Alfred Street, Milsons Point, Sydney, NSW 2061.
Colour separated in Switzerland by Photolitho AG, Zürich. Printed and bound in Italy by Grafiche AZ, Verona.

10 9 8 7 6 5 4 3 2

British Library Cataloguing in Publication Data available.

ISBN 1 84270 316 1

This book has been printed on acid-free paper

Tom had just watched a film on television. It was all about
pirates. "I wish I had a pirate ship to play with," he thought.
Then he had a brilliant idea. "I'll make one myself," he said.

"All I need to do is to collect a few things from around the house. I know just where to start," he said and he opened the door to the cupboard under the stairs.

Tom found two things that would be useful for a pirate ship. By looking at both pictures can you spot the difference between them and see what Tom has taken? One of the things would make a perfect mast.

Next, Tom went into the utility room. It was always in a terrible mess and there were plenty of things to choose from.

Can you spot the things that are missing?

Next Tom went into the kitchen. His mum had just finished making cakes and the smell made him hungry.

He took one cake for himself as well as four things for his pirate ship.

Then Tom went into the garage.
"There it is," he said, when he saw the police car he thought he had lost.

"But that's not what I need right now," and he took four more
things for his pirate ship.

Outside in the garden, Tom wondered what he might find that would be useful.

He collected six objects for his ship.

Next, Tom went upstairs to his sister's bedroom. It was full of interesting, lovable, fluffy, things.

He took four things altogether. One of them would look great
on a pirate's shoulder.

When Tom got to his own bedroom he remembered that his mother had asked him to tidy it up.

But he had no time for that now. He took nine objects for his pirate ship – six of them looked very much the same.

Although Tom had collected quite a lot of things he went into his father's study. He knew there would be lots of interesting things there.

He took five things altogether.

Finally Tom went up into the attic. It was full of hundreds of
different things. There was a broken television, a pair of skis
and the high chair that Tom had used when he was a baby.

There were also lots of old fashioned things like his
grandfather's gramophone, a top hat and an old sword which
Tom's dad said had been used in a famous battle.

This time Tom only took three things for his pirate ship.
Then he had everything he wanted.

He went to his room and using his imagination he built…

…the most incredible pirate ship. As you can see he used everything he collected from around the house.

If you want to be absolutely sure of where everything came from, turn to the next page.

THE CUPBOARD

1 box

1 broom

THE UTILITY ROOM

1 pair of boots

1 umbrella

1 t-shirt

1 coat hanger

THE KITCHEN

1 banana

2 spoons

1 tea-towel

THE GARAGE

1 ball of string

1 shoe box

1 flower pot

1 wheel

THE GARDEN

3 pegs

1 croquet mallet

1 umbrella stand

1 handkerchief

TOM'S SISTER'S BEDROOM

1 parrot

1 t-shirt

1 belt

1 felt pen

TOM'S BEDROOM

6 skittles

1 teddy

1 rocket

1 section of rail track

TOM'S FATHER'S STUDY

1 pair of scissors

1 roll of sticky tape

1 sheet of newspaper

1 ruler

1 piece of white paper

THE ATTIC

1 chandelier

1 broken doll

1 curtain

"That wasn't difficult," said Tom. "But there's more to do. Soon I will be sailing to find hidden treasure. But I need a crew. How good are you at spotting more things? If you can find everything on the next page, you can join the crew. But hurry, we are sailing at dawn."

If you found everything, congratulations and welcome aboard! But before we sail, I have one last question for you. Somewhere hidden in this book is the name of the ship. If you can find it, I will make you captain. So, start looking and good luck!

CAN YOU FIND?

 A mouse and a tennis ball in each picture?

CAN YOU SPOT?

THE CUPBOARD

1 candle
1 paint roller
3 spiders
1 walking stick
1 football

THE GARAGE

1 skateboard
1 apple-core
1 funnel
1 pair of oars
1 sledge

TOM'S BEDROOM

1 telephone
1 paper boat
1 snake
1 butterfly net
1 cork

THE UTILITY ROOM

1 sponge
1 frog
1 boat
1 loose button
2 pairs of rubber
  gloves

THE GARDEN

1 flag
1 kite
7 animals
1 rake
1 straw

TOM'S FATHER'S STUDY

1 calculator
1 elastic band
1 box of matches
1 drawing pin
1 paper clip

THE KITCHEN

Half a lemon
1 snail
1 elephant
1 oven glove
1 knife

TOM'S SISTER'S BEDROOM

1 giraffe
1 chair
3 rabbits
1 saddle
1 car

THE ATTIC

1 shepherd
3 light bulbs
1 umbrella
1 padlock
1 jack-in-the-box

More Andersen Press paperback picture books!

What Kind of Monster?
by Mark Birchall

Helpful Henry
by Ruth Brown

Up in Heaven
by Emma Chichester Clark

War and Peas
by Michael Foreman

Charlotte's Piggy Bank
by David McKee

The Wrong Overcoat
by Hiawyn Oram and Mark Birchall

Super Dooper Jezebel
by Tony Ross

Bear's Eggs
by Dieter and Ingrid Schubert

What Do You Remember?
by Paul Stewart and Chris Riddell

What Did I Look Like When I Was a Baby?
by Jeanne Willis and Tony Ross